Grayslake Area Public Library District
Grayslake, Illinois

1. A fine will be charged on each book which is not returned when it is due.

2. All injuries to books beyond reasonable wear and all losses shall be made good to the satisfaction of the Librarian.

3. Each borrower is held responsible for all books drawn on his card and for all fines accruing on the same.

Danny's Garden

written and photographed
by
Mia Coulton

Danny had a garden.

Everyday he watered

his garden.

Everyday he asked

Bee to help.

Bee just sat in the

red chair and watched.

Everyday Danny pulled weeds from his garden.

Bee just sat in the red chair and watched.

One   day,

Danny   saw   a   sign

by   his   garden.

"Bee's   fruits   +   vegetables"

Bee's
fruits+vegetables

He saw Bee selling

his fruits and vegetables!

Danny yelled at Bee,

"No fair!

I did all the work.

All you did was watch."

Danny saw another sign.

It was much better!

Bee's
fruits+vegetables

from
Danny's Garde